A Columbia Pictures Presentation

The Adventures of

STUART·LITTLE™

Based on the screenplay by Gregory J. Brooker
and M. Night Shyamalan

HarperTrophy®
A Division of HarperCollins*Publishers*

COLUMBIA PICTURES PRESENTS A DOUGLAS WICK AND FRANKLIN/WATERMAN PRODUCTION A FILM BY ROB MINKOFF GEENA DAVIS 'STUART LITTLE' HUGH LAURIE AND JONATHAN LIPNICKI
CO-PRODUCER JASON CLARK MUSIC BY ALAN SILVESTRI EXECUTIVE PRODUCERS JEFF FRANKLIN AND STEVE WATERMAN BASED ON THE BOOK BY E.B. WHITE SCREENPLAY BY GREGORY J. BROOKER AND M. NIGHT SHYAMALAN
PRODUCED BY DOUGLAS WICK DIRECTED BY ROB MINKOFF DISTRIBUTED THROUGH SONY PICTURES RELEASING COLUMBIA PICTURES

www.stuartlittle.com

Contents

1

Little, Not Big

George Little woke up in a very good mood. Today was going to be a great day. It was the day he was getting a brother.

"I'm going to play ball with him. I'm going to wrestle with him. I'm going to teach him how to spit!" George said excitedly. The bus pulled up, and he started to climb on. Then he remembered the most important thing of all.

"I want a little brother," he told his

parents before the bus doors closed. "Not a big brother."

"Okay!" they called, waving good-bye. Little did George know how seriously they would take his words.

Later that morning, Mr. and Mrs. Little sat in the playroom of the orphanage, watching the children. They wanted to choose somebody who was perfect for George.

All of a sudden, the Littles heard a voice. They looked down, and standing between them was a sweet-faced mouse wearing an orphan's uniform. The mouse's name was Stuart.

"Benny can do handstands," he said, pointing to one of his friends.

2

Two Votes "No"

Snowbell, the family cat, was in the kitchen when the Littles came in. He heard them, but he kept on eating, because that was what he liked to do best. Then he smelled something that made his whiskers twitch and his tail stand straight up.

Snowbell smelled a mouse.

He dashed around

the corner and gulped Stuart into his mouth.

"Drop him!" screeched Mrs. Little, her eyes wide.

"Spit him out right now!" yelled Mr. Little, stamping his foot.

Confused, Snowbell obeyed, and dropped Stuart onto the carpet. But the Littles kept scolding.

"Don't ever harm Stuart! He's one of the family now!"

That didn't make any sense at all to Snowbell. Mice were food. Even if they were wearing jackets, like this one.

Just you wait, thought Snowbell.

Just then, George got back from school, and ran down the hallway.

"Is he here?" cried George, his face pink with excitement. "Is my new brother here?"

"George," said Mrs. Little, "this is Stuart . . . your new brother." George looked around. Then he looked down. There at his parents' feet was a mouse, dressed in a uniform.

The mouse stuck out a tiny paw.

"You . . . you look somewhat like a mouse," said George.

"I am a mouse," said Stuart.

A mouse? His new brother? George did not know what to think. "I have to go!" he told his parents, heading for the basement.

"Is it just me," asked Stuart, "or did he seem a little disappointed?"

3

A Little Party

Mr. and Mrs. Little could see that Stuart was not fitting in. So they decided to throw a party for him.

"We'll have the family over . . ." said Mrs. Little.

". . . to meet our new son!" said Mr. Little.

The Littles were warm, friendly people with kind hearts. They came to the party with all kinds of gifts—skis,

a bicycle, a bowling ball, even a baseball that had once belonged to Mr.
Little's great-grandfather. Everything
was much too big for Stuart, but he
didn't mind. He knew the Littles were
trying to welcome him.

"This is the nicest party I've ever been
to," he told them. "In the orphanage we
used to tell fairy tales of finding our
families and having a party like this."

14

"I don't know much about families," Stuart went on. "But this must be the nicest family in the world. And now I know—fairy tales do come true."

Mrs. Little dabbed at her eyes with a handkerchief. "Now you're a Little, too," she said to Stuart, "and this is *your* house. And every Little in the world can find the Little house."

"George," his Uncle Crenshaw said, "why don't you take your brother outside and toss around that baseball?"

George stared at his relatives. "Are you all nuts?" he cried. "Bicycles! Skis? Mice don't ride bicycles! They don't ski! And they don't throw baseballs around!"

"He's not my brother! He's a mouse!"

he said, stomping out of the room.

Stuart wondered if he would ever fit in. He thought about his real parents and wondered if he would fit in better with them. So, he asked the Littles to help him find his real family. That was where he belonged.

The next morning, Mr. and Mrs. Little went to see Mrs. Keeper at the orphanage. Mrs. Keeper told the Littles that finding Stuart's parents might not be possible. "It's very difficult to track down mouse families," she said. "They're not good with paperwork."

"Please look into this for us . . ." said Mr. Little.

". . . and for Stuart," added Mrs. Little. "It would mean so much to him."

Mrs. Keeper thought the Littles were the strangest people she had ever met. At the same time she couldn't help liking them.

"I'll see what I can do," she said.

4

Upstairs, Downstairs

Meanwhile, it was turning into a very bad day for Snowbell. First Stuart asked him to play. Fat chance! Then Monty, one of Snowbell's alley cat pals, jumped through the kitchen window and started looking for food. Snowbell rushed after him in a panic. He did not want Monty to see Stuart. But just as Monty was about to leave, he noticed a wiggling tail in a box of crackers on the counter. He knocked the box over, and out came Stuart!

"Hello. You must be a friend of Snowbell's. I'm Stuart," he said politely.

"Aren't you going to run?" asked Monty.

"Why?" asked Stuart.

"Because you're a mouse," said Monty.

"I'm not just a mouse," said Stuart. "I'm also a member of this family."

"A mouse with a pet cat?" Monty asked. "That's the funniest thing I ever heard!" He rolled over laughing.

"I guess it is pretty funny," said Stuart, laughing too.

Enraged, Snowbell flew at Stuart with his sharp claws extended.

"Oh, dear," murmured Stuart. He turned and ran, squeezing under the door to the basement and rolling down the stairs until the floor stopped him.

"What are you doing here?" George snapped.

For a moment Stuart couldn't answer. He looked around. There were miniatures everywhere. There were cars,

trucks, houses, even a railroad . . . all exactly Stuart's size!

"Did you build all of these?" asked Stuart.

"Me and my dad." George was painting a tiny picket fence. He didn't look up.

"Wow!" said Stuart. "Is that a train?"

"What's it look like?" said George.

"Can we play with it?" Stuart asked. "Please, please, please?"

Stuart lay down on the train tracks

as if he were tied there. George couldn't resist. He started the locomotive and it whizzed down the tracks, heading straight for Stuart.

The instant before it reached him, Stuart leaped out of the way. "Ta da!"

Laughing, George stopped the train and applauded. Stuart was pretty daring!

"Hey! I have an idea," George said. He took out a red roadster and set it down next to Stuart. "Hop in," he said.

Stuart sat in the car, suddenly overcome by his feelings. For the first time since he'd arrived, he felt he was fitting in with his new family.

He looked around the wonderful room. "What's that?" he asked, pointing to a model ship on the worktable.

"That's the *Wasp,*" said George. "My dad and I were building her, but . . . I decided to stop."

"How come?" asked Stuart.

"There's this big boat race in Central Park," said George. "I thought I could enter her. But the other kids have store-bought boats . . . and they're bigger."

"The boats?" asked Stuart.

"No, the kids," said George. "I'm too little for a race like that," he mumbled.

Stuart knew how it felt to feel small and scared. "Little!" he exclaimed. "You're not little. Not to me."

"What if she lost?" George asked.

"At least she'll have tried," Stuart said. "C'mon. Let's get started."

It was a very surprised Mr. and Mrs.

Little who found the boys a few minutes later.

"I'm helping George finish the *Wasp* for the next race," Stuart told them.

"That's . . . that's wonderful!" said Mr. Little. "When is it?"

"Two days," said George, looking pale.

Stuart could hardly wait to get to work. "We'll be ready," he said.

Outside the house, Snowbell watched the Littles through the basement window. "I've got to take care of that mouse for good," he mumbled, and crept away.

5

Stuart, Ahoy!

Two days later, Stuart and George were standing at the pond in Central Park with Mr. and Mrs. Little. There were people all around them, and six very big, very fancy boats already in the water.

"See?" George said to Stuart. "This is what I was telling you about."

"Oh, dear," Stuart gulped. But he knew they had no time to waste. "We'd better get started!" he said.

They were checking the boat's remote control when Anton Gartran strolled by with the *Lillian B. Womrath,* a big, expensive boat with more controls than a rocket launcher. Anton was always picking on George at school.

"I'm glad you're here, George," said Anton. "Because somebody's gotta finish last, know what I mean?"

The starter called out the one-minute warning, and George handed Stuart the remote control.

"Hang on to this for a second," he said.

"Aye, aye," said Stuart. But the remote was so much bigger than Stuart that he stumbled backward, almost getting trampled by the crowd.

And the remote went flying.

Stuart picked himself up quickly, but not quickly enough to stop the large foot in the heavy boot that was about to step on the remote.

"Look out, sir!" he cried—too late.

The remote was ruined forever. Stuart stood next to it, horrified.

"George! I . . . It was completely my fault," said Stuart miserably. "I just couldn't—"

He was interrupted by a sharp

cackle. Anton Gartran was pointing at the shattered remote and laughing.

"Ten seconds!" called the starter.

George's eyes filled with tears.

"There'll be other races, George," said Mr. Little, trying to comfort him.

"No, there won't," said George. He turned and walked away from the pond as if he never wanted to see it again.

"All boats to their marks!" called the starter. "Ready . . . Set . . . GO!"

The horn blared. There were shouts and cheers as the race began. Then the race starter announced, "Sails are full and . . . is that a *mouse* on that boat?"

George and his parents ran back to the pond, pushing their way through the crowd in amazement.

Stuart, aboard the *Wasp,* was hoisting her sails. The *Wasp*'s remote didn't work, so Stuart would simply operate her the old-fashioned way—he would sail the boat himself.

Once the sails were up, the *Wasp* glided away from shore, helped by a friendly gust of wind.

Stuart was on his way!

On shore, the Littles watched proudly as Stuart closed the distance between the *Wasp* and the other boats.

At the halfway point, he steered so deftly that he cut ahead of all the other boats—even the *Lillian B. Womrath*.

The Littles cheered.

Anton was so furious, he used his remote control to send the *Womrath* directly into the *Wasp*. The big boat hit the *Wasp* hard, and Stuart was nearly thrown overboard.

But he recovered. The *Wasp*'s mast was now entangled in the *Womrath*'s rigging, so Stuart quickly climbed up the mast and untangled the boats.

Anton grinned. "I hope that mouse can swim!" He steered his boat toward the *Wasp*. Just in time, Stuart dodged the *Womrath*.

Suddenly, Anton lost control and his boat careened into the rocks. He screamed and worked his remote furiously, but it was no use. The *Wasp* flew past the *Womrath* and crossed the finish line—in first place!

As Stuart approached the shore, he heard one of the spectators ask, "Who *is* that mouse?"

"That's no mouse," said George Little. "That's my brother." He lifted Stuart into the air while everyone around him cheered.

6

Two Stout Mice

That evening the entire Little family gathered to celebrate George and Stuart's victory. They cheered when Stuart and George came down the stairs carrying their sailing trophy, and clamored for a photo of Mr. and Mrs. Little and their sons.

"You four look great together!" said Uncle Stretch as he took the picture. He didn't have to tell them to smile— they were smiling already.

This is the happiest moment of my life, thought Stuart.

And then the doorbell rang.

When Mr. Little opened the door, he found two tiny figures looking up at him. Mice. Well-groomed, well-dressed mice.

"Mr. Little?"

"Yes?"

"My name is Reginald Stout, and this is my wife, Camille," said the

mouse in the suit. "We're sorry to interrupt this lovely affair, but we're looking for Stuart."

"Are you friends of his?" asked Mr. Little.

"No," said Reginald.

"Fellow yachtsmen?" Mrs. Little asked.

"We're his parents."

"George, Stuart," said Mr. Little, who was getting very upset, "I think we need to talk to the Stouts alone."

As soon as George and Stuart were gone and the guests had left, Mrs. Little turned to the mouse couple. "I think you should understand something," she told them, her voice shaking. "Stuart is very happy here. He's . . ."

". . . one of the family," finished Mr. Little.

"I know you think you're Stuart's family," Reginald said, "but he'll never really be family, trust me. No offense, but . . . you're human. We're mice. You may not understand the difference, but Stuart does, I guarantee."

"We let him go once because we loved him, but we couldn't afford to support him," said Camille. "Now it's your turn."

The Littles didn't know what to say. How could they keep Stuart from his real family? It was terrible to lose him, but it wouldn't be right to keep him.

Mrs. Little, who was trying very hard not to cry, went to tell Stuart and George that Stuart would have to go with the Stouts.

Blinking back tears, Stuart went to pack a bag.

"This stinks!" cried George, storming down to the basement. But a few minutes later, when Stuart was outside hugging the Littles good-bye, George came running down the front steps of the house.

"Wait, Stuart!" He ran up to his brother. "I want you to have this," he said, setting the little red roadster down on the street.

"George . . . I couldn't," said Stuart.

"I want you to," insisted George.

"My, my, this is one fine automobile," said Reginald admiringly. He jumped into the roadster and gunned the engine. Camille climbed into the front seat next to him.

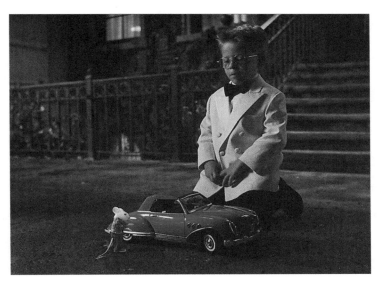

"Come along, son," called Reginald. Numbly, Stuart obeyed.

He waved sadly to George through the rear window of the car. And then they were gone.

1

Mousenapped?

The next few days were miserable for everyone. Reginald and Camille tried to make their mouse house comfortable for Stuart. Camille even fed him her best

bits of garbage. Stuart knew they meant well, but somehow they just didn't feel like family. Every night he stared out his tiny bedroom window, and wished he could be with the Littles. He even found himself missing Snowbell.

As for the Littles, they missed Stuart terribly. No matter how they tried to cheer themselves up, they felt lonely without him.

Just when everybody was feeling their absolute worst, Mrs. Keeper came to visit.

"I have something to tell you," she said. "Stuart's parents had a terrible accident. They were in a grocery store, in the canned-soup section, and a pyramid of cans fell . . . and they were crushed."

"How terrible!" cried Mrs. Little. "How's Stuart taking it?"

"He doesn't know," said Mrs. Keeper.

"No one's told him?" asked Mr. Little. "Isn't he going to wonder when they don't come back?"

"But they've been gone for years," said Mrs. Keeper.

"Stuart's parents came and took him away three days ago," said Mrs. Little.

"No," said Mrs. Keeper slowly, "Stuart's parents died *years* ago. I just told you."

"Are you sure?" asked the Littles.

Mrs. Keeper nodded.

The Littles jumped to their feet. "We'd better take this up with the police," said Mr. Little.

Snowbell, who had been listening to the conversation, sat up with alarm.

"Take what up with the police?" asked George, who appeared in the doorway.

"Stuart's parents," said Mr. Little. "They weren't really his parents at all . . ."

". . . and we think your brother has

been kidnapped," finished Mrs. Little.

"What?" George shouted.

Snowbell slunk out of the room. A few minutes later he and Monty were in the alley, reporting fearfully to Smokey, the alley cat leader, and the rest of the alley cats.

"They know we hired the Stouts to trick Stuart! I'm in big trouble!"

"All right, all right!" said Smokey. "New plan. Spread the word," he told the alley cats, "and make it snappy. That mouse Stuart gets scratched tonight."

Snowbell crept away, dreading what was to come.

8

Cats and Mouse

Smokey's message got to Reginald and Camille quickly. Later that night, they woke Stuart and told him to get dressed—they were going for a ride.

Yawning sleepily, Stuart climbed into the backseat of the roadster. It was very quiet in the car—until Stuart heard Camille crying.

"What's wrong, Mom?" he asked,

but his innocent question only made her cry harder.

Which made Stuart feel terrible.

"Mom!" he said. "I'm not angry at you anymore for giving me up when I was a baby. I'm a Stout again. I'll always be here to take care of you." He patted her shoulder with his tiny paw.

"'Cause that's what families do, right? They take care of each other."

Camille wailed uncontrollably. "Tell him the truth!" she ordered, hitting Reginald with her bag. Reginald pulled over. Then Camille blew her nose and Reginald confessed. They weren't his real parents. They were fakes. Smokey

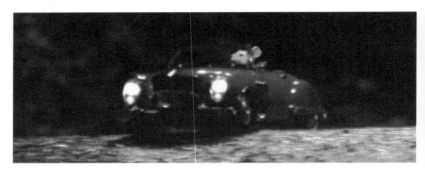

had forced them to do it. He was a powerful cat and he wanted to get rid of Stuart, and the Stouts were afraid to cross him.

Stuart was shocked.

"You lied and cheated? You took me away from the Littles just when we were all so happy?"

"Yes," they admitted, ashamed.

He jumped out of the car and paced for a moment.

"That's why I've been feeling so sad!" he cried. "That's why I keep thinking about them! I'm not a Stout! I'm a Little! I'm Stuart Little!"

His voice was so loud that Reginald clapped a paw over his mouth. "Shhh, Stuart! Listen to us! You're in terrible, horrible danger!"

Then they all heard it—a loud, bloodthirsty *meeowww* coming their way on the midnight wind. It was an awful sound.

"As your fake father," Reginald said to Stuart, "I order you to run!"

Stuart hopped into the red roadster and backed it up. "Good-bye, Fake Father! Good-bye, Fake Mother!" he called as he drove off.

"Good-bye, Fake Son!" they answered as they ran away.

Stuart sped through the quiet city streets and into the park.

Soon I'll be home, he thought. *I just have to get through the park.* He came to a fork in the road, and stopped the car. Which way should he go? Then all at once he saw them—three of the meanest-looking street cats he had ever seen.

"Well, well," hissed one of them. "You must be Stuart."

"Actually," said Stuart, "I must be going." He slammed into reverse and backed off into the trees, startling the cats so they scattered. Then he skidded off a ledge. The car turned in the air, and plummeted down a ravine straight into a drainage culvert.

It was a big, spooky tunnel, but Stuart didn't care. All he cared about was getting out of there, fast. He hit the gas hard. The roadster shot into the dark just out of the reach of the cats.

Stuart barreled down the culvert. Suddenly he realized the tunnel was ending. But it was too late to stop, and the car flew through the air.

Splash!

Stuart and his car landed in the water. Stuart struggled to the surface, gasping for air, when suddenly his suitcase bobbed up next to him in the water.

Hmmm, thought Stuart. *Just big enough for a raft.* He hoisted himself aboard. The cats were standing on the

edge of the culvert, yowling in disappointment. Stuart waved good-bye as he floated away.

But he hadn't gotten far when he heard a low rumbling sound. Stuart looked in front of him and saw a grating lit from above. Below the grating was a waterfall that sounded as big as Niagara Falls to Stuart. He had to do something. He'd made it this far, hadn't he? So just before his suitcase went over the waterfall, he jumped onto the grating and held on tight.

As he pulled himself upward, he wondered if he would ever make it back to the Littles' house.

9

Cat and Mouse

A few minutes later, wet and bedraggled, Stuart climbed up over the curb from the storm drain below. All he wanted was to go home. He reminded himself, "Every Little can find the Little house."

As he turned away from the curbside, he saw something that made him the happiest he had ever been. There, across the street, was the Little house.

He raced up the steps and sailed in

through the mail slot. He looked around for his family, but the only one there was Snowbell.

"Where is everybody?" Stuart asked, looking around the empty living room.

Snowbell knew that the Littles were desperately trying to find Stuart. All day they had been knocking on doors and telephoning their neighbors. Even now, they were out putting up "Missing" posters in the park. But Snowbell also knew that this might be his last chance to get rid of Stuart. So he decided to lie.

"Movies," said Snowbell. "Ever since you left they've been celebrating. They're having the time of their lives!"

His eyes glinted with malice.

"Celebrating? Celebrating what?" asked Stuart.

"Well, they were just so happy to get rid of you," said the cat.

"That's a lie!" cried Stuart.

"The proof's right up there," said Snowbell, pointing to the Little family portrait on the mantel. Stuart's face had been cut out.

"They did that right after you left," said the cat. "Didn't want to look at your face anymore."

The truth was that the Littles had cut Stuart's picture out so they could use it on a poster.

But Stuart didn't know that.

He believed Snowbell. And his heart broke.

With tears streaming down his furry little face, he ran out of the house and headed back to the park.

He had nowhere else to go.

Just as Stuart got to the park, the Little family arrived back home. They'd put up hundreds of posters.

"Now all we have to do is wait until somebody calls to tell us where Stuart is," George said. Mr. and Mrs. Little looked at each other worriedly.

"If we don't find Stuart, it's going to break his heart," Mrs. Little said.

Nearby, Snowbell mumbled to himself, "Ah, the kid will get over it."

Later that night, Monty told Snowbell Smokey's plan for getting rid of Stuart.

"Why do we have to scratch him out?" Snowbell asked. "Hunting and scratching out aren't really my strengths."

"Smokey himself sent me to get you. You gotta come!" Monty replied.

"Take it easy!" Snowbell huffed as they ran through the park with the other alley cats. "The only exercise I get is rolling over." As the cats continued

on, Snowbell stopped to catch his breath and noticed Stuart sitting in a tree.

10

A Little at Last

Stuart sat in a tree, thinking sad thoughts as the night deepened. A chilly wind rippled the surface of the water. Just then, he heard a voice.

"Stuart! What are you doing up there?"

"Oh, I'm settling in," Stuart said.

Snowbell climbed the tree and sat next to him. "Look, Stuart, if I were you, I'd relocate."

"It's not so bad," Stuart replied. "At least it's got a view."

Suddenly Stuart and Snowbell heard the other cats. "Hey, look," Stuart said, "it's your pal Monty. Hey Monty! Up here!" he yelled.

"What are you doing?" hissed Snowbell.

Below, the cats began congratulating Snowbell for finding Stuart.

Snowbell grabbed Stuart by the collar and rushed further up the tree.

"Stuart, I lied, okay? George loves you. They're all nuts about you!" he confessed.

Stuart couldn't believe his ears. The Littles loved him after all!

Unfortunately, the cats had caught up to them. Stuart and Snowbell were surrounded in the tree.

"What's going on here?" Smokey asked.

"Look, I want to call this whole thing off," Snowbell replied.

"Snow, what are you doing?" Monty asked. "C'mon, he's just a mouse!"

"He's not just a mouse. He's family!" Snowbell said.

For a moment, Smokey and the other cats were shocked. "Okay," Smokey said at last. "Scratch them both!"

Stuart jumped, but not far enough. He dangled from a limb above a branch loaded with very large, very hungry-looking cats.

"Oh dear!" he said and closed his eyes.
Crack!

Snowbell had thrown his weight onto the branch beneath Stuart.

"Look out!" yelled a voice. The branch broke and the whole gang fell—right into the lake!

Snowbell rushed to help Stuart, but he was suddenly face to face with Smokey.

"Where do you think you're going?" Smokey sneered.

Slowly Snowbell backed away from the angry cat, but there was no escape.

"Hey, Smokey. Did you forget something?" It was Stuart, standing right behind Smokey! He held back a long branch like a whip. He let the branch go, and it knocked Smokey right out of the tree!

Smokey went sailing into the water below, where he landed near the other cats. Cold and wet, they all struggled onto the shore.

"I . . . uh . . . let's get out of here!" Smokey said, and with that he led the street cats away.

Snowbell started walking home with Stuart on his back. Before long the Little house was in sight.

Snowbell leaped onto the window ledge and Stuart climbed off his back. Snowbell looked at Stuart and sighed.

"Thanks," Stuart said, hugging Snowbell tight.

"Don't mention it . . . ever!"

Snowbell replied.

At that moment George, asleep in the living room, woke and glanced at the window. A strange and wonderful sight met his eyes. Stuart, his beloved little brother, was hugging Snowbell the cat, right on the windowsill!

I'm dreaming, thought George, rubbing his eyes. He got up. Stuart waved. Snowbell meowed.

I'm not dreaming! George realized. Then he started yelling "Stuart! Stuart!"

Mr. and Mrs. Little hurried into

the living room. They threw open the window.

"I knew you'd come back!" cried George.

"How did you manage it, Stuart?" asked Mr. Little.

Stuart paused as he looked at the beaming faces of the Littles. "Every Little in the world can find the Little house," he said.

And Stuart knew he was finally where he belonged.